# Kylie Kangaroo's Karate Kickers

by Barbara deRubertis • illustrated by R.W. Alley

KANE PRESS / NEW YORK

# Alpha Betty's Class

Alexander Anteater

Bobby Baboon

Corky Cub

Dilly Dog

Eddie Elephant

Frances Frog

Gertie Gorilla

Hanna Hippo

Lana Llama

Izzy Impala

Jeremy Jackrabbit

Kylie Kangaroo

STAR of the BOOK

Maxwell Moose

Nina Nandu

Oliver Otter

Polly Porcupine

Quentin Quokka

Rosie Raccoon

Sammy Skunk

Tessa Tiger

Umma Ungka

Victor Vicuna

Walter Warthog

Xavier Ox

Yoko Yak

Zachary Zebra

Alpha Betty

Series Editor: Juliana Hanford
Book Design: Edward Miller

Library of Congress Cataloging-in-Publication Data

deRubertis, Barbara.
Kylie Kangaroo's karate kickers / by Barbara deRubertis ; illustrated by R.W. Alley.
p. cm. — (Animal antics A to Z)
Summary: Kylie Kangaroo is taking lessons at Koora Koala's karate club and uses
a lucky kerchief to learn to break a brick.
ISBN 978-1-57565-332-7 (library binding : alk. paper) — ISBN 978-1-57565-323-5 (pbk. : alk. paper)
[1. Karate—Fiction. 2. Kangaroos—Fiction. 3. Koala—Fiction. 4. Alphabet.]  I. Alley, R. W.
(Robert W.), ill. II. Title.
PZ7.D4475Ky 2011
[E]—dc22    2010021822

ISBN 978-1-57565-375-4 (e-book)


5 7 9 10 8 6 4

Kane Press

An imprint of Boyds Mills & Kane, a division of Astra Publishing House

**www.kanepress.com**

Printed in China

Animal Antics A to Z is a registered trademark of Astra Publishing House

Kylie Kangaroo was keen on keeping fit.

She liked to hike.

She liked to fly her kite.

And she liked to play kickball with the
other kids at Alpha Betty's school.

KA-POW!

One day, Koora Koala stopped to watch the kickball game.

When it was finished, Kylie walked over. "Hi, Koora!" she said. "What's up?"

Koora smiled. "Kylie, I've been thinking.
I like the way you KICK when you play kickball.
Would you like to take karate lessons at my club?"

"Oh, yes!" said Kylie.
"I think I would like karate!
I'd like to learn some kicking tricks.
And I'd LOVE to learn to break a brick!"

"Okey dokey!" said Koora.

"Here's a free ticket to join my karate club.

With those kickers, you'll pick up karate quickly."

Kylie worked hard at Koora's karate club.
She did have powerful kickers.
But Kylie's kicks often missed the mark.

Her tricks did not click.
And she could NOT break a brick.

SMACK.

BRICKS FOR BREAKING

SMACK.

SMACK.

"Ouch! Ouch! OUCH!" cried Kylie
as she whacked a brick.
"I am not a karate kid.
I am a karate klutz."

Koora Koala spoke to Kylie.

"Take my lucky kerchief, Kylie.
I was wearing it when I was crowned
King of the Karate Kickers!"

Koora handed Kylie the kerchief.

"Just tie this around your neck," he said.

"It will help you do kicks and tricks.
It will help you break STACKS of bricks."

"Thank you, Koora!" said Kylie.

Now Kylie worked even HARDER at Koora's club.
Her kicks and tricks started to click.

It looked as if Koora's kerchief
was working!

But Kylie still had to learn how to break a brick.

She practiced her kicking for weeks and weeks.

One day, Koora was waiting outside the club for Kylie.
"I think today's the day, Kylie," said Koora.
"I think you're ready to break a brick!"

"Woo-HOOO!" Kylie cried.
She streaked into the club like a rocket.

Koora picked up the lucky kerchief Kylie had dropped.
His eyes twinkled as he tucked it into his pocket.

Inside, Kylie picked out a big, thick brick.

Then she took a quick look at herself
in the mirror. She was shocked!

"Oh, NO!" Kylie cried.
"I've lost Koora's lucky kerchief!"

"It's okay, Kylie," said Koora.
"You can do it without the kerchief!"

Still, Kylie panicked.
She looked at the brick.
Then she quickly gave it a kick.

SMACK.

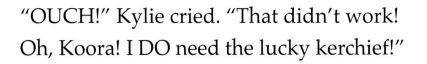

"OUCH!" Kylie cried. "That didn't work!
Oh, Koora! I DO need the lucky kerchief!"

"Keep your cool, Kylie," said Koora.
"Take your time. And think!
You've worked hard for weeks and weeks.
The key to breaking the brick isn't the lucky
kerchief. The key is YOU!"

Kylie took a deep breath.
She carefully set up the big, thick brick.
And she looked at it for a long time.

Then Kylie spoke. "You know, Koora,
I think I CAN break this brick!"

*KER-WHACK!*

Kylie cracked the brick in two!

Koora Koala cheered. "Way to go, Kylie!
What a kick! Someday you'll have a black
belt in karate."

Kylie Kangaroo kicked her kickers higher
than she'd ever kicked before.

Just then Kylie looked at Koora's pocket.
"Koora! YOU have the lucky kerchief!"

Koora smiled. "Yes, Kylie," he said.
His eyes twinkled brightly.

Kylie Kangaroo gasped.
"You've had the kerchief all along!"
Then she began to laugh.

"Koora," said Kylie, "you were right.
I didn't need the kerchief.
I broke that brick ON MY OWN!"

Then Kylie Kangaroo kicked her kickers
SO high, she came CLUNKING down.

KER-

And she broke a whole STACK of bricks
. . . without even trying!

**THUNK!**

# STAR OF THE BOOK: THE KANGAROO

## FUN FACTS

- Home: Most kangaroos live in Australia.
- Family: Kangaroos belong to the family called *macropods* (meaning "large foot"). Female macropods all have pouches where they keep their babies after they are born.
- Travel style: Kangaroos are the only large animals that only move by hopping. They can hop forward, but not backward!
- **Did You Know?** Kangaroos use their large legs and feet for FAST hopping, AMAZING leaping, and POWERFUL kicking.

## LOOK BACK

Learning to identify letter sounds (phonemes) at the beginning, middle, and end of words is called "phonemic awareness."

- The word *kangaroo* has a *k* sound at the <u>beginning</u> of the word. Sit on a chair and listen to the words on page 5 being read again. When you hear a word that <u>begins</u> with the *k* sound, clap your hands over the top of your head and say the word.

- The word *trick* has a *k* sound at the <u>end</u> of the word. Listen to the words on page 15 being read again. When you hear a word that <u>ends</u> with the *k* sound, carefully kick up your feet and say the word.

## TRY THIS!

**Kylie's Lucky Kerchief Words**

- Fold a sheet of paper into 8 squares (fold in thirds lengthwise; then fold across into thirds). Cut the squares apart into "lucky kerchiefs." (You will have one square left over.) *
- Use crayons to write the following letters on the kerchiefs: Write the consonants *l, r, s, t* with a **black** crayon. Write the vowels *a, i, o* with a red crayon. Write *ck* with a green crayon.
- See how many words you can make by placing a **black consonant** at the <u>beginning</u>, a red vowel in the <u>middle</u>, and the green *ck* at the <u>end</u>. Sound out each combination. What does each word mean?

* A printable, ready-to-use activity page with 8 "lucky kerchiefs" with letters written on them is available at: www.kanepress.com/AnimalAntics/KylieKangaroo.html

(Words you can make: lack, lick, lock, rack, rick, rock, sack, sick, sock, tack, tick, tock)